MW00961544

Naomi Nash

The Drama Noodle

by Jessica Lee Anderson

illustrated by Alejandra Barajas

PICTURE WINDOW BOOKS
a capstone imprint

Published by Picture Window Books, an imprint of Capstone.
1710 Roe Crest Drive, North Mankato, Minnesota 56003
capstonepub.com

Text copyright © 2023 by Jessica Lee Anderson
Illustrations copyright © 2023 by Capstone

All rights reserved. No part of this publication may be reproduced in whole
or in part, or stored in a retrieval system, or transmitted in any form or by
any means, electronic, mechanical, photocopying, recording, or otherwise,
without written permission of the publisher.

Library of Congress Cataloging-in-Publication Data
Names: Anderson, Jessica Lee, 1980- author. | Barajas, Alejandra, illustrator.
Title: The drama noodle / by Jessica Lee Anderson ; illustrated by Alejandra
Barajas.
Description: North Mankato, Minnesota : Picture Window Books, an imprint
of Capstone, 2023. | Series: Naomi Nash | Audience: Ages 6-8 | Audience:
Grades 2-3 | Summary: Naomi and her friends Emma and Taylor are
signed up for drama camp, but Naomi would rather spend her time saving
snakes—until she realizes that the two can be combined in the form of an
interview with a local television station.
Identifiers: LCCN 2022029331 (print) | LCCN 2022029332 (ebook) |
ISBN 9781666349443 (hardcover) | ISBN 9781666349481 (paperback) |
ISBN 9781666349528 (pdf)
Subjects: LCSH: Snakes—Juvenile fiction. | Day camps—Juvenile fiction.
| Acting—Juvenile fiction. | Best friends—Juvenile fiction. | Friendship—
Juvenile fiction. | CYAC: Snakes—Fiction. | Day camps—Fiction. |
Acting—Fiction. | Best friends—Fiction. | Friendship—Fiction.
Classification: LCC PZ7.A53665 Dr 2023 (print) | LCC PZ7.A53665 (ebook)
| DDC 813.6 [Fic]—dc23/eng/20220705
LC record available at https://lccn.loc.gov/2022029331
LC ebook record available at https://lccn.loc.gov/2022029332

Designed by Kay Fraser and Jaime Willems

All internet sites appearing in back matter were available and accurate
when this book was sent to press.

Printed and bound in the USA. POB 5195

TABLE OF CONTENTS

CHAPTER 1

PUPPY TRAINING TROUBLE

Snake fact #1: Most snakes have teeth, but only venomous snakes have fangs. Snakes don't have teeth like molars because they don't chew their food like herbivores.

My best friend, Emma, helped me tie fishing line around a dark-brown snake. It was tricky to tie a knot around the snake's head. Good thing it was made of rubber!

"I don't think your plan is going to work, Naomi," my older brother said as he looked on from the couch.

"It's worth a try. Weren't you busy reading or something?" I said.

Nolan rolled his eyes at me and picked up his book again. He normally liked reading

about space, but this time he'd checked out a
snake field guide from our library.

I still couldn't believe the change in my
brother. Nolan used to think snakes were slimy
and scary. But then I'd had the idea to start
a club to help snakes in our neighborhood—
if they were nonvenomous, that is. We left
venomous snake saving to the experts.

Ever since our snake rescue club had taken
off, Nolan had been doing a lot of research.
Now he was acting like some kind of expert.

I went back to helping Emma. We were
supposed to be meeting up with Taylor, our

neighbor and friend, to train her puppy. The fake snake was a key part of our plan.

Emma added an extra knot to keep the fishing line from coming undone. "This thing sure looks real," she said.

"I agree . . . even if I've never seen a black mamba in person," I said.

I picked up my notebook of snake facts. I'd been keeping it for a couple of years now. It was filled with pages and pages of interesting things I'd learned about snakes. I flipped to snake fact #134.

"Did you know that black mambas got their name because their mouths are a bluish-black color?" I said. "They open their mouths as a warning sign."

"The way a cottonmouth does if it feels threatened?" Nolan asked.

"Exactly," I said.

"The cottonmouth has a white mouth, right?" Emma asked.

Nolan answered before I could. "Yes, and that's how it got its name too."

"I want to draw a picture later to compare a black mamba to a cottonmouth," Emma said.

Like I kept a notebook of snake facts, Emma carried a sketchbook with her everywhere. She was always drawing in it. Her art was so good!

"There are some interesting differences between the two. Black mambas are in the elapid family of snakes, but cottonmouths are pit vipers—" I started to say.

My brother interrupted. "Naomi, you're showing off."

Nolan's words stung like the hangnail I pulled at. He was right. Apart from Mom— a veterinarian at the Austin Exotic Animal Hospital and trained wildlife rehabilitator—I was used to being the snake expert in the family.

Emma gave me an understanding smile. "I want to hear more about it later, Naomi. For now, I think we're ready."

She wrapped the rubber snake around her arm like a piece of jewelry. Unlike a real black mamba, which could grow up to fourteen feet, this toy was only about four feet long.

Emma tugged at the fishing line to make the head of the snake move like it was talking. "*Let'sssssss* go," she said in a silly voice. "Taylor and Marshmallow are waiting for *usssss.*"

I laughed.

Nolan popped off the couch, knocking his book to the ground. "I've got to see this."

"We'll be back in a bit!" I called.

I knew Mom was at work—Saturdays were busy days at the clinic—but Dad didn't answer, so I walked down the hallway to their bedroom. Dad was in their closet, hanging up Mom's work scrubs. He had headphones over his ears.

I waved to get his attention. "We're going next door to hang out with Taylor," I said.

Dad lifted his headphones. "Have fun and be safe," he said, playing the air guitar.

I giggled. My dad could be so funny. I waved goodbye and then Emma and I headed out the front door. Nolan followed behind.

Taylor and her puppy, Marshmallow, were waiting for us on her front porch. As soon as Taylor saw Emma's rubber-snake-wrapped arm, she shrieked. Marshmallow barked in reply.

"Don't worry! The snake is fake!" I yelled.

Nolan snickered. "This is better than television," he said under his breath.

Taylor sat down and took several slow breaths. I understood that some people didn't like snakes, but they really, really scared my neighbor. Marshmallow wagged her fluffy tail and plopped into Taylor's lap, trying to kiss her.

"I didn't mean to scare you," Emma said.

"I wasn't prepared for that thing to look so alive," Taylor said. Her voice was shaky.

"It's made of rubber. No way we'd ever handle a super-duper venomous snake like a black mamba," I said.

Taylor took another couple of slow breaths.

"I don't think you're helping, Naomi," said Nolan.

My brother was right. I should've toned down the venom talk. I tried to make things better.

"You'll find black mambas in Africa, not a place like here in Austin, Texas," I added. "Anyway, do you want to get started?"

Taylor nodded and stood up. She had been teaching Marshmallow to "leave it" so the puppy wouldn't get into things that she shouldn't. The fake snake had been my idea. Dogs could be too curious if they came across a snake on a walk or in the backyard.

I thought of snake fact #187: *Since snakes don't have limbs, spines, horns, tusks, or claws, the only form of defense they have is to bite.*

Emma unwrapped the snake from her arm. "Here we go," she said. She held one end of the fishing line and tossed the rubbery black mamba. It flopped to the grass near her feet.

"Leave it," Taylor said to Marshmallow, but it was too late. The puppy pounced on the fake snake and nipped it with her sharp teeth. "Leave it, Marshmallow! Please don't chew that awful thing!"

Marshmallow ignored Taylor, but a moment later, the puppy got distracted by a girl riding her bike at the end of the street. I quickly snatched the rubber snake.

"Can I do the next snake toss?" Nolan asked, taking it from me. "Scene one, take two."

He tried to fling the snake but somehow didn't let go of the string fast enough, and the snake yo-yoed back to him. Even Taylor laughed when the rubber tail thumped against his chest.

"What are you doing?" a voice asked. The girl who'd been biking down the street rode up on the sidewalk near Taylor's front yard. She looked close to Nolan's age, like eleven or so.

"Uh, nothing," Nolan said.

The girl jumped back when she saw the rubber snake in the grass.

"I thought it was real at first too, but it's fake. We're training my dog to avoid snakes," Taylor said. She glanced down at Marshmallow. "It's not going well."

The girl leaned her bike against the curb. "Gotcha. Aren't you part of a snake club, Nolan?"

"Uh . . . not really. It's mostly something the little kids do," Nolan said.

Something the little kids do? He's a part of the club! I thought.

I shot my brother a look, but he was staring down at his feet. His cheeks turned so red it looked like he'd gotten an instant sunburn. Emma caught my eye and shrugged.

"That's too bad. I think it's a good idea," the girl said. She righted her bike. "Well, I guess I'll see you all around."

"Who was that?" Taylor asked after the girl biked off.

"Her name is Isla. She's in my grade at school. I didn't think she even knew my name," Nolan said.

"Word must be spreading about our club," Emma said. "We had a ton of views after I posted the video of us rescuing the rough earth snake that the cat brought inside."

Emma pulled out her cell phone and showed us the video on the club website her mom had designed. The website looked awesome!

Emma had even drawn our logo and added our mission statement. *WE HELP SNAKES. WE HELP PEOPLE. WE HELP OUR NEIGHBORHOOD.*

"You've had a thousand hits!" Taylor said. "You'll be famous soon."

"Wow!" I said, wondering what it would be like to be famous. We could help a whole lot more snakes and animals that way!

I reached down and grabbed the rubber snake from Marshmallow, then tossed it back into the yard. Right as Marshmallow looked ready to pounce, I said, "Leave it."

Marshmallow did *not* leave it. She slipped out of her harness and raced after the fake snake. She grabbed the rubbery thing in her mouth and shook it.

"Oh, Marshmallow," Taylor said. She caught up to the puppy and put her harness back on. "We have a lot more training to do." She turned to face us. "That reminds me. I have kind of a weird thing to ask you all . . ."

CHAPTER 2

DRAMA CAMP

Snake fact #2: Venom is basically toxic snake spit that
stuns or kills prey. Venom can help break down food for
snakes to digest.

"What's up?" I said. "You can ask us
anything." Emma and I had been friends for
years, but we'd recently become better friends
with Taylor too.

Emma nodded in agreement. She gave
Marshmallow a rubdown and then retrieved
the rubber snake from her.

"My uncle registered me for Acting Explorers
Camp. It's supposed to start on Monday, but it
might get canceled if more kids don't sign up."
Taylor looked hopeful. "Do you want to join
me? It would be a lot more fun with friends."

"Is that like drama camp?" Nolan asked.

"Yeah. It's for two weeks, but it's just a day camp," Taylor said. "You'd be in the age group up from us, though. I think that section for older kids is full. Sorry."

"You don't need drama camp anyway," I told him. "Your acting skills are already good. I almost believed you when you said you weren't part of the club."

Nolan blushed. "I don't know why I said that." He looked in the direction Isla had biked.

Taylor turned to Emma and me. "What do you think?" she asked.

"I've only done an art camp before, but taking an acting class together would be fun and different," Emma said. "I'll ask my mom if I can go."

I hesitated. I did *not* like talking in front of big groups. Acting was not for me. Not to mention, I usually preferred some kind of science or nature camp. But I didn't want to let Taylor down.

"I'm not sure I'll have the time, but I'll check in with my parents."

Nolan shot me a look. "I'm sure Mom and Dad will say yes," he said.

Taylor looked at me hopefully, and I nodded. Maybe learning some acting skills would help me overcome my fear of public speaking.

Camp could help if we really become famous, I thought. I'd need to be able to talk to a group if I was going to share the importance of snakes with everyone.

"I'll ask tonight," I promised.

Nolan was right about my parents saying yes, and after dinner, Mom went online to sign me up for Acting Explorers Camp.

"I hope this doesn't get in the way of the club," I said. "There are lots of snakes to rescue."

"I think this will be a great opportunity for you to grow and challenge yourself, Naomi," Mom said.

"And I'll have some peace and quiet to read and research while you're at camp," Nolan said.

He'll know more about snakes than me if he keeps this up, I thought. "But isn't the snake stuff something only the little kids do?"

Nolan's face turned red. "I think the club is fine, but . . . never mind. It's complicated."

How was I supposed to respond to something like that?

Emma called a little later to say her mom signed her up too.

"Is it bad I don't really want to spend every day for the next two weeks at drama camp?" I asked her.

Emma didn't answer right away. "I think it will be fun," she finally said. "Plus, the camp isn't all day. We'll still have time to swim and do other stuff."

"True, and most importantly, to save any snakes that might need our help," I said.

I wasn't sure what to wear the first day of camp on Monday. Would the other kids be wearing costumes or fancy dresses? Eventually I decided to wear my usual shorts and favorite T-shirt. It had the words *Danger Noodle* with a funny drawing of a cobra nestled in a bowl on the front.

Since he had a flexible schedule, Dad had volunteered to drive us to camp. Taylor met us on the sidewalk in front of our house that morning.

"Do you think Marshmallow will be okay all day without me?" she asked.

"I'm sure she'll miss you, but she'll be okay with your uncle," I said.

A few minutes later, Emma walked up carrying her sketchbook. She wore a shirt with bright yellow, red, and blue dots and a red skirt. It was the perfect outfit for an artist going to drama camp.

"You look fantastic!" I said.

"I'm so happy you two decided to come to camp!" Taylor said.

"It'll be fun to hang out together," I agreed.

Since Emma had her sketchbook, I ran inside to grab my snake notebook before we left. It might come in handy. Then we all piled into the car.

As Dad drove, he cleared his throat and started speaking in a theater-like voice. "I was once a young actor when I was your age, girls. You're looking at Jack himself—from *Jack and the Beanstalk* of course."

"Really?" I asked. It was hard to picture Dad onstage at eight or nine years old.

"The kid who was supposed to play Jack got sick, so I filled in for him. Good thing the play was a comedy because my acting was a joke," Dad said, laughing.

I worried I wouldn't be able to act *at all*. The thought of stepping in front of strangers made my heart race like a sidewinder.

"Do you think I should stay home in case someone calls and needs help with a snake problem?" I asked.

"Not at all," Dad said. "Your brother and I have it covered."

I frowned. *So much for that tactic.*

We pulled up in front of the Austin Kids Playhouse. Dad parked, then led the way inside to get us all signed in. There was a woman waiting at the registration desk.

"Welcome! I'm Alexandra, the director here at Acting Explorers Camp," she said. "You three kiddos will be in room one act."

"Thanks! We're excited to be here," said Taylor.

Some of us are, I thought, wondering what I'd gotten myself into.

When we got to room one act, our camp leader was waiting for us. She looked younger than most of my teachers at Austin Bats Elementary.

"Welcome!" she said. "I'm Divya. We're going to have a blast exploring drama!"

Emma, Taylor, and I introduced ourselves. There were two other kids there too—Jordyn and Oliver. I waved hello, and Oliver gave me a shy wave back.

Jordyn looked me over like she was sizing me up. "Do you like snakes or something?" she asked, pointing at my shirt.

"She *loves* them," Taylor said. "Naomi and I are neighbors. She's always trying to save snakes and bring them home."

Jordyn made a disgusted face.

"Snakes aren't gross," Emma said, placing her hands on her hips.

"Emma helps Naomi," Taylor continued. "They made a little club."

Little club? I thought. I thought Taylor *wanted* to be part of things. Maybe she didn't join our rescues, but she helped in her own way, like making flyers.

"We'll do a warmup activity in a moment, but first, I want to go over some rules," Divya said. "Number one: Always respect each other. I want everyone to feel safe, especially as we explore acting and performance skills."

I was used to being safe when rescuing snakes, but how dangerous could acting be?

"Be you and be creative!" Divya continued. "We'll put on a performance at the end of camp, and your family members are invited."

A performance? Acting in front of strangers was bad enough. Now the crowd would be even bigger? I was not looking forward to standing up in front of everyone, especially Nolan.

Divya looked at all of us. "Lastly, be careful when we go outside. There's been a report of a snake near the koi pond. The director doesn't think it's poisonous, but it's still best to be safe."

I almost raised my hand to share snake fact #280: *Snakes are venomous* not *poisonous. Poison is swallowed, and venom is injected.*

But then I thought of what Nolan had said the other day. I didn't want to seem like a know-it-all show-off.

Emma looked over at me and raised her eyebrows. I knew we were thinking the same thing. With a snake sighting, drama camp had just gotten a whole lot more interesting!

CHAPTER 3

CAMP MYSTERY

Snake fact #3: Snakes don't get sick from their own venom!

Divya gathered us all in a small circle, then went to check the audio equipment.

Jordyn turned to me and pointed at my shirt again. "What does *danger noodle* even mean?"

"Some people call snakes noodles because of their shape and all," I explained. "This is a venomous cobra, so it's a danger noodle. Get it?"

"Not really," she said, scooting back.

"I think your shirt is cool," Oliver said.

"Do you like snakes?" I asked him.

Oliver nodded. "I went to the Animal Farm and Snake World Zoo at the start of summer. I wonder what type of snake is by the pond."

"I bet it's a plain-bellied water—"

"Who cares what kind of snake it is?" Jordyn interrupted.

"Snakes do a lot of good for our environment!" I felt my voice rising.

"And they really aren't scary once you learn more," Emma added.

Before I could respond, Divya returned. "Okay!" she said, clapping her hands. "Let's get started."

We moved in closer, though Jordyn stepped away from me.

"Did you know that acting is really the art of reacting? It's the way someone responds onstage to speech or action. Improv—or improvisation—is acting without a script or plan. It helps you to listen, think on your feet, and take some creative risks," Divya said.

No script? I wasn't sure if I could act even *with* a script! Drama camp was even harder than I'd thought.

Divya wiggled her hands. "Let's do some improv by pretending you're a snowflake falling to the ground to the speed of the music you hear. Starting in three, two, one. Go!"

It was hard to pretend it was cold—summer in Texas was *hot*—but I decided to give it a try.

A Mozart symphony played at first, so I swayed to the sound of a violin. Oliver sort of did the same. Emma and Taylor twirled around. Jordyn busted out some ballerina-snowflake

moves. She was a good performer, even if she had a bad attitude about snakes.

Next, the music switched to hip-hop. I moved my arms like a snowflake bouncing in the breeze. Oliver jumped around. Divya even snowflake-danced with us.

"All right," Divya said. "Now pretend you're a fly zipping along to the beat of the music."

I roamed around the room. By the time country and jazz played, all of us were laughing and out of breath.

"I need to wear more comfortable clothes tomorrow," Emma whispered to me.

When it was break time outside, I grabbed my notebook. I couldn't wait to explore.

"Let's go search for signs of the snake," I said.

Emma nodded and slipped her sketchbook into her bag. We waited for Taylor to catch up.

"Actually, I'll see you two later," Taylor said to us. She walked over to the picnic benches where Jordyn sat eating her snacks.

"So much for fun with friends and hanging out together at camp," Emma said.

"Yeah. What did you think about Taylor's club comments earlier?" I asked.

Emma pulled a granola bar out of her bag and offered me half. "I think she's trying to impress Jordyn."

It reminded me of how Nolan had acted with Isla. "I think you're right," I said.

I shared my bag of grapes with Emma as we walked. There was lots of room to explore outside. Flowers grew all over the grounds.

I heard a twig snap behind us and turned around. Oliver ducked behind a tree.

"Are you spying on us?" I joked.

"Uh, I figured you knew where the koi pond was. You're looking for the snake too, aren't you?" Oliver said.

I smiled. "Want to join us?"

Oliver nodded eagerly. Soon we found the koi pond near a small shed. Someone else was already there. I recognized Alexandra, the director from registration.

"Hi, guys. How's your first day?" she asked.

"Great," Oliver said. "Is the snake out here?"

"That's what I'm checking on," Alexandra said. "I recently found two snakes around the area, but one disappeared. I'm afraid one of the big koi might've eaten it."

She pointed to the pond. A large orange-and-white fish swam to the surface, opening and closing its mouth.

Usually, snakes hunted fish, not the other way around. I scribbled a note in my notebook to research more about koi later.

"Is it a plain-bellied water snake?" I asked.

"No, it's smaller, like a garter snake," Alexandra said.

Talking about snakes helped me feel more comfortable. "Did it have a stripe or a checkered pattern?" I asked. I opened my notebook to show some pictures of garter snakes.

"Definitely the checkered one," the director said. She pointed to snake fact #80: *Checkered garter snakes have yellowish stripes like other garter snakes, but they have a black checkered pattern. They're found in the southwest all the way to South America.*

I closed my notebook. "Ooh! Checkered garter snakes are gentle and gorgeous. I've never seen one in person before."

The director stood up and stretched. "You really know a lot about snakes."

Emma handed the director a homemade business card she'd drawn. "We created a snake rescue club. Naomi's parents are wildlife rehabilitators. We've saved some snakes that have gotten stuck different places—one on a glue trap and one in a pool skimmer cover."

"That's really something," the director said. "You should meet my friend, a naturalist and a reporter. She's coming here tomorrow to help me finish replacing this old netting with a safety fence. It should help keep snakes, critters, and you kids safe."

"That would be awesome!" I said.

I really hoped we could meet her. Drama camp might be worth it after all if she could help make our club famous . . . I just needed to overcome my fear of public speaking first!

CHAPTER 4

DRAMATIC NATURE

Snake fact #4: Some venomous snakes have hollow fangs. They're like needles that inject venom from a special gland. Other snakes have grooved fangs. They drip venom out when the snake holds on to bite.

After break, we listened to a song called "The Wild Zoo." It had a fast beat and rhythm.

"This is the song we'll be dancing to for the performance. You can be any animal you'd like," Divya said. "Let's get into character."

"I bet she's going to be a snake," Jordyn said to Taylor, pointing at me.

I scowled. I *did* want to be a snake, but I didn't want to give Jordyn the satisfaction of being right.

Taylor giggled with Jordyn, then the two of them started to claw the air.

"Are you puppies?" I asked them, thinking of Marshmallow.

Jordyn stared at me like I was speaking a different language. "No! We're wolves."

Taylor broke out of character to add, "I hope Marshmallow is doing okay without me." She started telling Jordyn all about her puppy.

I could tell Emma was trying to keep the peace. "Marshmallow is one of the most adorable puppies ever." Then she stood on one leg, the other bent and resting on her kneecap. "Can you tell what I am?"

"A flamingo?" I guessed.

Emma nodded. I had no idea what to be, so I did the same thing until my leg got tired.

Oliver was pretending to be a bat. I joined him for a bit. I still had no idea what animal to be for our performance. After the way Jordyn had made me feel, there was no way I could

be a snake. I pictured myself slithering off the stage as everyone pointed and laughed. So much for drama camp helping me get over my fear.

By the time camp ended for the day, I was exhausted.

While we waited for Dad to pick us up, I turned to Taylor. "How come you ditched us earlier? I thought you wanted us to come to camp so we could spend time together."

Taylor looked surprised. "Sorry, I didn't mean to . . . Jordyn is just so confident and cool."

Emma cleared her throat. "I think Naomi and I are confident and cool too."

"I didn't mean it like that. Of course you are!" Taylor said.

I wasn't so sure about me being confident, especially when it came to performing. I decided to let it go, though. There was nothing wrong with Taylor wanting to make a new friend.

Dad had homemade pretzels waiting in the car for us when he arrived. "Thought I'd add a little twist to your day," he joked.

"Twist! I get it. Thanks, Dad," I said, sinking my teeth into the soft, salty dough.

"Yes, thanks. You're such a good baker, Mr. Nash," Emma said with her mouth full.

Taylor nodded as she took a big bite. "Mmmhmmm."

I picked off a chunk of salt that had fallen onto my danger noodle shirt. "Did anything exciting happen while I was gone?"

"You mean besides baking pretzels from scratch?" Dad said, laughing. "I'll let Nolan tell you about a weird phone call we got today."

The pretzel sat heavy in my tummy. *Sounds like I missed something important*, I thought.

When we got home, Taylor needed to take Marshmallow outside. "Can't wait to hang out tomorrow. Bye!" she said, racing off.

"Say hi to Marshmallow for us!" I called after her.

Emma had plans with her mom. "Call me later to fill me in about the phone call," she said.

I nodded, then headed inside. I found Nolan on the family computer in our living room.

"What happened while I was gone?" I asked, walking over to him. "Dad said you got a weird phone call?"

Nolan turned around in the chair to look at me with wide eyes. "You're not going to believe this, Naomi. A green anaconda escaped from a zoo, and they want our help—"

"How in the world did an anaconda escape?" I interrupted.

Snakes sometimes got out of their enclosures, but an anaconda? They were some of the largest and heaviest snakes in the world!

I flipped through my notebook to find snake fact #124: *The green anaconda is a type of boa that lives in South America. They lurk in places like swamps and marshes. An adult anaconda can grow more than twenty-nine feet long and weigh more than 500 pounds.*

I had a hard time imagining something that weighed twice as much as our dad sneaking out of its enclosure. "What zoo?"

Then I looked at Nolan's face. He was doing his best to hold back his laughter.

I sighed. "You're joking, aren't you?"

"I had you going there for a moment, Naomi! Maybe I worked on some acting skills today too," Nolan said after a fit of laughter.

I rolled my eyes at my brother, then went into the kitchen to pour myself a glass of water. The salty pretzel had made me thirsty.

"Were you in on this prank?" I asked Dad after I'd taken a sip.

"Not me. Promise," Dad said. "We really did get an interesting phone call, just not from a zoo about an escaped giant snake."

I looked over at my brother, who'd come into the kitchen too. "Are you going to tell me what it was about or not?" I demanded.

"An alligator sighting."

"An alligator in Austin? Are you joking again?" I asked.

Nolan shook his head. "No joke. I did some research, and there have been quite a few alligator sightings in Austin over the years. A couple of them were probably illegally released, but others might've traveled here from east Texas. They're native to that area. They can travel long distances and sometimes get swept up in flood waters."

It wasn't a snake fact, but I still added details about alligators to my notebook. "What did you guys end up doing?"

"We reported the sighting to Texas Parks and Wildlife," Dad said. "They're the experts when it comes to a situation like this."

I didn't say it out loud, but I was glad my dad and brother hadn't rescued a snake while I was at camp. Then I felt bad. If a snake needed help, it shouldn't matter if I was there or not.

"The fact that someone thought to call us shows me that Emma is right. Word is spreading about our club," Nolan said.

His comment reminded me of earlier. "Emma mentioned our club to the camp director today. She wants to connect us to her friend who's a naturalist and a reporter."

"That'd be awesome!" Nolan said.

"I really hope it works out so we can keep sharing how important snakes are." I told them about the snake at the koi pond. "Do you think it's possible a koi could eat a snake?"

"Maybe," Nolan said. "Let's look it up."

The three of us headed to the living room to do some research on the family computer. I learned koi were omnivores. They ate things like seeds, plants, insects, and even small frogs. And sure enough, we came across a video of a large koi slurping down a small garter snake.

"Talk about drama in nature," Dad said.

When Mom came home from work, we showed her the video too.

"I suppose it's sometimes a matter of size whether you eat or get eaten," Mom said. She pulled out her cell phone. "Let me show you a picture someone shared with me at work today."

Nolan scooted away. "Please tell me it's not some gross surgery photo."

"I'll spare you from that . . . for now at least," Mom said with a grin.

I looked at her phone. A hawk was lying on a trail as if injured. When I zoomed in on the photo, I saw the reason why. A snake had wrapped itself around the hawk's wings!

Based on snake fact #83, I recognized the type of snake—a coachwhip. It had long features and tan scales that made the snake look like a whip.

"One of my coworkers spotted this while hiking. The hawk chose a meal that was too big to eat. The snake likely wrapped around the hawk's wings and legs in defense so the hawk couldn't fly off. Once the standoff ended, they both escaped," Mom said.

"It's another instance where the predator becomes the prey," Dad said in a dramatic voice.

It reminded me of the theater voice he'd done in the car that morning when he'd talked about being in a play as a kid.

"Dad, how did you get through playing Jack in *Jack and the Beanstalk*?" I asked.

"One line at a time," Dad said. "Why do you ask?"

I shrugged. I didn't want to tell my family about my acting jitters—especially not with Nolan there. I knew he'd give me a hard time.

"There's a big performance at the end of drama camp and—"

"Oh, how exciting!" Mom interrupted. "You better believe we'll be there!"

Dad beamed.

"I won't even bring a book to read during your performance," Nolan said.

I forced a smile. If I didn't have the jitters before—which I totally did—I *definitely* had them now.

CHAPTER 5

SAD ELEPHANT

Snake fact #5: Fangs can be at the front of a snake's mouth or in the back part of a snake's mouth. A snake called the stiletto snake has side fangs.

Mom had to work at the clinic the next morning, so she offered to drop Emma, Taylor, and me off at drama camp on the way.

"How can I get Marshmallow to stop chewing stuff?" Taylor asked Mom on the ride there.

"She might be teething," Mom said. "Puppies go through that phase the same way kids do. Make sure you have lots of toys and bones for Marshmallow to chew on. When you see her chewing something you don't want her to, tell her to drop it and redirect her with something that's okay for her to chomp on."

I smiled proudly. Mom knew so much about animals. Someday, I wanted to be a veterinarian like her. Or maybe I wanted to work at a zoo.

"Did you know that snakes lose teeth and then regrow them throughout their lives? Their teeth and fangs can get stuck in prey when they eat," I said.

"I didn't know that," Emma said. "That's really cool."

"Really weird," Taylor said.

"Weird *and* cool," I said. We didn't say much else on the way there. I wondered if Taylor was going to be better about hanging out with us today. I hoped so.

"May your day be filled with lots of fun drama," Mom said after she signed us in at drop-off.

"Yours too," I responded without thinking. "Well, you know what I mean." Drama at a vet's office would *not* be good. "Have a good day, Mom."

Mom winked at me. "Of course. Dad will pick you up later."

As we made our way to our classroom, I didn't see anyone near the koi pond. *Too bad camp is about to start*, I thought. I really wanted to explore the area.

Oliver waved at us when we walked in. He was wearing a snake shirt like I had yesterday, only his was different.

"Remember how I said I went to the Animal Farm and Snake World Zoo?" He pointed to the logo. "I got this shirt there."

Taylor groaned. "We're in drama camp! Why can't I escape snakes?" She moved over to where Jordyn sat at the table.

"I like your shirt," I said. I liked Oliver too. He was fun and friendly.

"Same," Emma said.

I walked over to Jordyn. She was wearing a shirt with Shakespeare's face on it, along with the quote, "All the world's a stage."

"I like your shirt too, Jordyn." I said, trying harder than yesterday to connect with her. "It's the perfect thing to wear to drama camp."

Jordyn flipped her hair back and smiled. "'And all the men and women merely players.'"

I had no idea what she meant by that.

"That's the rest of the quote from Shakespeare, right?" Emma asked.

"Yes," Jordyn said. "Drama is my life."

"Mine too," Taylor agreed.

Is she just trying to impress Jordyn? I wondered.

"I'd say drawing is my life," Emma said.

"Rescuing animals is mine, especially animals like snakes—"

I didn't get to finish my thought because just then Divya walked into the room. She clapped her hands to get our attention.

"Welcome to our second day of camp! As we warm up today, be in the moment," she instructed. "Don't give in to fear, and don't ever, ever worry about failing.

Easier said than done, I thought. Divya had *just* said not to worry about failing, but that's exactly what I was worried about.

"We'll spend the next few minutes walking around the room," Divya continued. "Change the way you move based on what emotion or character I call out. We'll start with . . . sad elephant!"

Huh? I thought.

Everyone else started playing along. Emma moved slowly and used her arm like a trunk. Then she dropped down into a sad elephant heap. Jordyn did the same thing.

I still felt confused, but I followed along.

"Bumbling Bigfoot!" Divya yelled.

I bumped into Jordyn as I took giant steps. "Sorry!"

Jordyn turned around and glared at me. "Watch it, snake girl."

I frowned, feeling hurt. *She might not like snakes, but why doesn't she like me?* I wondered.

After a few more walks around the room, we moved on to our next activity.

"We'll be playing a game of charades next. Using only gestures, you'll try to get your teammates to guess a word. Let's divide up into two teams," Divya said.

"Emma, come join Taylor and me," said Jordyn.

Emma looked over at me. After a moment, she said, "No thanks."

Her hesitation made me wonder if my best friend didn't want to be on my team.

It's no big deal, I said to myself. We'd created a snake club together, after all. That was the team I really cared about, not some charades game.

"You can join their side if you want," I said to Emma. "Oliver and I can be a team."

Oliver sucked in a deep breath. I wondered if he was feeling left out too.

"Really?" Emma asked.

I used my acting skills to hide my hurt feelings. "Sure."

Emma hesitated another moment. Then she joined Jordyn and Taylor on the other side of the room.

Divya held out a box with some cards in it. "The charade cards are all objects. Naomi, you're up first!"

I reached into the box and pulled out a card. Hula-Hoop! How was I supposed to act that out?

Divya set the timer for thirty seconds. I wasted a few of them thinking about what to do. Then I held my hands up and rocked on my legs back and forth like I had an invisible Hula-Hoop around my waist.

"Dance! Funny dance? Snake charmer?" Oliver guessed.

The other team laughed, including Emma.

I kept trying, but I couldn't get Oliver to guess Hula-Hoop before the timer buzzed. I looked down at my feet. I felt like a complete failure.

Emma, Taylor, and Jordyn were up next. They seemed to read each other's minds and guessed the word "blanket" right away. They all high-fived each other.

At least I figured out Oliver's word— guitar—when it was his turn. That one was easy with all the air guitar my dad played at home.

I got slightly better as the game went on, but Oliver and I didn't stand a chance. The other team kept laughing and cheering.

"You should join their team next time," I told Oliver after we lost.

He smiled at me. "Winning isn't what matters. I had fun."

That made one of us. Winning would've at least helped me feel better in the moment.

When Divya announced that it was break time, Emma was still talking with Taylor and Jordyn. It felt like yesterday when Taylor had chosen to hang out with Jordyn instead.

"I'm going to go see what's happening at the koi pond," I said quietly. Time was ticking, and I really wanted to meet the naturalist reporter."

"Can I come with you?" Oliver asked.

"Sure," I said.

The heat felt good but intense as we walked the grounds. Oliver was quiet, which I appreciated. I wasn't up for talking much.

As we got closer, I spotted Alexandra, the camp director, by the pond. Another woman was standing next to her. She looked familiar, though I wasn't sure why.

"You've got to come see this!" Alexandra called, waving at us.

CHAPTER 6

KOI POND
RESCUE

Snake fact #6: Snakes like vipers have fangs that fold up against the roof of their mouths when they're not biting something. Gaboon vipers have the longest fangs at around two inches!

Oliver and I rushed over. We stopped near where the director held a section of the netting.

"No way!" I exclaimed.

A small snake was wrapped up in the netting. I recognized the checkered pattern and yellowish stripes right away. The checkered garter snake was more gorgeous in person than in any photo!

"I shouldn't have been so careless when I started to pull up the netting yesterday," Alexandra said. "It must've gotten trapped."

Oliver knelt to get a better look. "I've never seen a snake outside in nature before."

"Most of the time, snakes go undetected," the woman next to the director said. "They're here, but we don't usually notice them until we interfere. Sort of like now with this netting."

Sounds like something Mom would say, I thought.

I looked around to see where Emma was. She would've loved this information, plus she would've taken some pictures. But there was no sign of her.

She must still be chatting with the other group, I realized. The group I didn't belong in.

"This snake is larger than the other one I've been seeing around. It sure is stuck," the director said, holding up the netting. "By the way, this is my friend Deborah Aston, the naturalist I was telling you about."

No wonder she looked familiar! I'd seen her on the news before! She hosted short videos for a segment called Feel Good Friday.

"I'm glad our future generation cares about misunderstood animals," Deborah said. She used some clippers, but the snake wriggled, making it hard to cut the netting.

"Can I help?" I asked. "I can hold the snake steady."

"That's a nice offer, but I don't want you to get hurt," Alexandra said.

A bite from a garter snake wasn't dangerous. It just needed to be washed with some soap and water after. I didn't want to cause any trouble, though, so I moved to the edge to grab the netting instead. My shoes squished into the muddy ground.

"I can keep this steady while one of you cuts and the other holds the snake," I said.

"Good thinking," Deborah said.

Oliver moved close to me to help lift the netting.

"That's making things easier," Alexandra said to us.

The snake continued to fight, so I moved my hand near its tail to keep the netting from flopping around.

Suddenly a horrible smell—like a combo of dead fish and rotten eggs—filled the air. Gross!

I thought of snake fact #292: *Snakes spray musk as a stinky form of defense.*

Oliver gagged. "It smells awful."

He was right. Looked like I'd be needing a whole lot of soap and water even though I hadn't gotten bit.

Less than a minute later, the snake was free. Deborah gathered it into her hands and walked it over to the shed area to release it.

I was sad that Emma wasn't there to have been part of the rescue. She would've loved seeing the snake's checkered pattern, even if the ordeal was stinky. I felt just like I had after the game of charades—awful. I hoped Emma was at least having fun with Jordyn and Taylor.

Before Oliver and I returned to class, Deborah handed me her card. "I'd love to send out someone from our station to interview your club. The news could use more feel-good stories with a positive message. Have one of your parents get in touch with me."

I was speechless. I couldn't believe this was happening!

"Thank you," I finally managed to say. "That would be amazing!"

Once again, I wished Emma was here. She'd given the director one of our cards already, but she could've given one to Deborah too. And I knew she would've had something smart and kind to say.

"Do you think I could join the snake club?" Oliver asked as we walked back.

"I'll have to talk to the rest of the group," I said. "It seems like you just had a stinky initiation, though."

Privately, I was worried. *After what Nolan said the other day and the way things are going with Emma, will our club even make it?*

"I understand," Oliver said. "Even if you don't want me to join, it's okay. It wouldn't be the first time I wasn't a part of things."

Oliver looked so sad when he said that. Sadder than any sad elephant during the improv warm-up.

"I'm glad I found a friend who likes snakes," I said.

Oliver looked up, and his eyes seemed cheerier. "My dad made me sign up for this camp so I'd make friends. I almost made a bet with him that he was wrong. Good thing I didn't. I'd owe him money."

I smiled when he said that. "My friend Taylor roped me into this camp, but she's hanging out more with other people than me."

I nodded to where Emma, Taylor, and Jordyn were hanging out near the picnic bench area.

When we joined the others, Jordyn lifted the neck of her Shakespeare-themed shirt to cover her face. "Were you two diving in the sewer or something?"

Taylor pinched her nose. Emma looked at me with wide eyes.

"We got musked by a checkered garter snake," I said, filling them in on the rescue mission.

Emma's eyes filled with tears. "You rescued a snake without me?" Without another word, she turned and ran inside.

"Emma!" I called after her, but she didn't stop. I finally caught up to her in the hallway.

"Why did you choose Oliver over me?" Emma asked.

"I didn't! I thought you chose Jordyn and Taylor over *me*," I said. "I thought I was doing you a favor since it seemed like you wanted to join them. I waited for you at break time, but then you never showed."

"I thought you might've been too busy with your new friend for an old friend like me," Emma said.

"No way I'd ever be too busy for you!" I insisted. "I felt the same way about you getting along with Taylor and Jordyn. I was trying to act like I wasn't upset, but I should've told you how I was feeling."

"I should've just talked to you instead of making guesses about what you were thinking." Emma wiped her eyes. "I'd give you a hug right now, but you smell terrible."

We both laughed and fist bumped instead.

When the other kids joined us, Jordyn acted like she was going to faint from the stench.

Divya clearly noticed it too. "How about we spend the rest of the day outside? It'll do us good to practice for the performance in some fresh air and to channel our zoo characters," she said in a nasally voice.

We found a shady spot, and Divya blasted out "The Wild Zoo."

"Inspiration is all around us!" she exclaimed. "Let's start thinking about our dance moves like pieces of a puzzle we're putting together."

I practiced being an alligator as we learned some dance steps. I thought about their strength and how they could adapt. I was so focused I almost crashed into Jordyn again. She waved her hand in front of her nose.

"What happens if we aren't up for performing next Friday?" I asked Divya. "I'm not sure I'm cut out for this acting business."

"The show must go on!" Divya said theatrically. "Seriously, though, I think it is important to do things that challenge us, so we'll grow."

That reminded me of what Mom had said when she signed me up for camp. I had a whole lot of adapting and growing to do if I was going to survive the performance.

CHAPTER 7

A SURPRISE PATIENT

Snake fact #7: Spitting cobras have holes in their fangs that they shoot toxic venom out of if they feel threatened.

Taylor and Emma kept their distance from me while we waited for Dad to pick us up. Not that I blamed them. The musk smell still clung to me even after washing up and airing out.

"I wish you guys could've seen the checkered garter snake," I said. "It was beautiful."

"No thanks," Taylor said. "And animals like peacocks are beautiful, not snakes."

"Did you know peacocks will fight snakes and eat them?" I asked.

Speaking of eating, my stomach grumbled. *I hope Dad has a snack with him,* I thought.

Taylor shook her head. "I like peacocks even more now."

"Snakes and peacocks are both beautiful," Emma said. She sketched a snake with a checkered pattern in her notebook. "I wish I'd gotten a picture of the garter snake earlier."

"We'll hopefully rescue another one someday . . . together," I said. I pulled out the card Deborah Aston had given me. "I met this naturalist and news reporter who wants to interview us soon. I need to talk to my parents to organize things."

"Us?" Taylor asked.

I paused, trying to get my words right. "Well, the snake club—"

"I can't wait!" Taylor interrupted. "I've always wanted to be on television!" She bounced up and down so hard she nearly fell off the curb.

Emma and I looked at each other. I wasn't sure what to say. Taylor wasn't technically a part of the club, but I didn't want to hurt her feelings. I knew how awful it felt to be left out.

Just then I spotted a familiar-looking SUV.

Why is Mom picking us up instead of Dad? I wondered. *Did I hear her wrong earlier?*

"Sorry for the delay," Mom said after signing us out. "I had to swing by the wildlife center. It's nearby, so I told Dad I'd pick you up."

I opened the passenger door and saw a small travel carrier. "Do we have a new patient?"

Taylor nearly fell off the curb all over again. "I'm not getting in if there's a snake inside!"

"The snake nearly drowned in a pool and is sick with a respiratory infection. It's not going anywhere for a while," Mom replied. "Plus, it's in a secure container. Trust me—I wouldn't take any chances on a snake getting loose, especially knowing how you feel about them."

Taylor fanned herself. "If I didn't need to get home for Marshmallow, I'd walk. It's bad enough that Naomi smells like a snake."

"C'mon, you'll be safe in the back seat with me," Emma said, opening the door.

Taylor hesitated a moment before sliding in. Emma plopped into the seat next to her.

Mom turned to look at me. "What's this about smelling like a snake?"

I told her about the checkered garter snake caught in the netting. I left out the part about Emma not being there with me.

Mom cracked the windows for some fresh air. "Musk is a great way for snakes to avoid fighting or using up their venom, but it sure does smell awful."

I held the container in my lap, making a note to add a fact about musk to my snake notebook when I had my hands free. As Mom drove, I peered inside the container. From what I could see, the snake was brown with blotches. It had a thick neck and an upturned snout.

"A drama noodle!" I exclaimed.

"A what?" Taylor asked.

"The snake is an eastern hognose! Some people call them drama noodles. If a hognose gets scared, it'll spray musk like other snakes, but it can also roll over and play dead. A hognose is an amazing actor. I'll have to show you some videos," I said.

"Uh, no thanks," Taylor said.

"It's not play acting now, is it?" Emma asked. She stretched forward to look over my shoulder.

Mom shook her head. "No, it's had some trauma. A worker found it drowning at the city

70

pool and brought it to the wildlife center. It must've been going for a drink but couldn't get out. The rescue center is at capacity, so a friend there called me," she explained.

I loved when Mom brought animals home to rehabilitate. She always taught me how to take care of them.

Taylor didn't share my enthusiasm. As soon as we got home, she jumped out of the SUV.

"Marshmallow is waiting on me!" she called as she ran off.

Emma came over to open the car door for me. "I texted my mom on the way home. She said it's okay to hang out at your house for a while. I mean, if you want me to."

"Of course!" I answered, cradling the carrier. Emma leaned closer to get a better look at the eastern hognose.

As soon as Mom opened the front door for us, we were blasted by the smell of chocolate. Yum! My stomach rumbled again.

"Brownies are ready!" Dad called from the kitchen.

"Be warned they're made with black beans," Nolan said. He was over by the computer again.

Mom led the way over to the terrarium we kept in the living room. She pulled the eastern hognose out of the carrier and inspected the snake before setting it into the enclosure.

"He just needs some rest and a little bit of care," she said. "Soon he'll be on his way."

The snake's tongue flicked out. He used his snout as a shovel to hide in the mix of sand and reptile-safe soil.

"I bet your acting skills aren't as good as my sister's," Nolan said to the hognose.

I smiled at my brother. It was a kind thing for him to say, even if he was wrong.

"We should call him Thespis," Dad suggested, coming into the room.

"Thespis?" I asked.

"He was an ancient actor," Dad explained. "He's the reason actors are called *thespians* to this day." He winked at Emma and me. "Speaking of, we're looking forward to seeing you thespians perform at the end of camp."

I changed the subject. "Thespis is a perfect name for a drama noodle."

Emma started sketching Thespis while I went to change and clean up. Then we all gathered in the kitchen for a snack. Dad passed out plates with large squares of black-bean brownies.

"Thanks, Mr. Nash," Emma said, digging right into hers.

I bit into mine. The texture was like fudge.

"I forgot to tell you—something exciting happened at camp today!" I said as I chewed. "Deborah Aston was there. She gave me her card and said the news station is always looking for an inspiring story. Do you think we could do a snake club interview for Feel Good Friday?"

"Wow, a chance to star in a performance and now this great opportunity! Way to go! I'll reach out to her for more information," Mom said, grabbing some milk from the fridge for us.

Talk about pressure, I thought.

"Taylor wants to take part in the interview," I blurted out. "And Oliver wants to join the club too. He's a kid from camp who likes snakes," I explained to my family. Then I turned back to Emma. "Do you think we should ask him to be a part of the interview?"

"Why not?" Emma said with a piece of chocolate on her lip. "The more the merrier."

Is she just acting, or does she mean that? I wondered.

CHAPTER 8

PREP TIME

Snake fact #8: Snakes have several teeth hiding out in their gums if they need to replace them, including fangs if the snake is venomous.

When I flipped on the living room lights, Thespis peeked his head out of the sandy soil.

"Morning, buddy," I said.

Thespis started zipping around like he was worried about something. It made me think of snake fact #156: *Some snakes are diurnal—they're quiet at night and more active during the day.*

Mom was sipping coffee in the kitchen with Dad when I went to find her. I poured myself a bowl of cereal and milk.

"Does Thespis seem restless?" I asked.

"That sounds like a song title. Thespis is restless!" Dad belted it out like a country singer.

"You're funny, Dad," I said, laughing. I was surprised his singing didn't wake up Nolan.

"Respiratory tract infections can make snakes feel uncomfortable, plus he's probably unsettled," Mom explained. "Do you think you can help me give him a shot after breakfast? The antibiotics will treat the infection."

"Sure." I didn't like shots, but I needed to toughen up if I wanted to be a vet someday.

Mom prepared the medication, then reached for Thespis in the terrarium. He flattened his head and neck, hissed, and curled up his tail.

"You look like a danger noodle, Thespis,"
I said.

"It's no surprise people think these snakes
are tiny cobras the way they mimic behaviors,"
Mom said.

Thespis struck at Mom as she picked him up,
but he never opened his mouth.

"He sure is living up to his name," she said.
"That was a bluff strike. He pretended to bite me
but just booped me with his nose."

I helped keep Thespis from curling up. Mom
quickly gave him a shot between the scales. With
all this stress, I expected him to roll over and
play dead, but he didn't. Thankfully he didn't
spray musk either! I couldn't smell yucky in front
of my campmates for a second day in a row.

Emma arrived as Mom was setting Thespis
back into the terrarium. Dad was driving us to
camp again that morning.

"Are you sure you're okay with Oliver and
Taylor joining the club?" I asked her.

Emma sighed. "I was afraid I'd lose you as my best friend. Then I thought about what Divya said in drama camp about not giving in to fear."

"I don't want to lose you either! It felt so wrong being at the koi pond without you," I said.

Emma smiled. "Let's make a deal. We stick together no matter what."

"Deal," I said, reaching out to shake her hand.

When we arrived at camp, Oliver greeted us wearing another snake-themed shirt. As much as I loved snakes, *I* didn't even have that many snakey shirts.

"You're welcome to help out with the snake club," Emma said to him.

Oliver looked like he was about to burst with excitement. "I'm so glad I came to this camp!"

By the middle of the morning, I wished it was nature camp instead. Divya kept making

us practice our zoo song for the performance again and again and again.

"Practice makes perfect!" she told us.

Ugh. I felt far from perfect as I tripped over my feet. My legs were getting sore from the alligator moves.

After what felt like forever, it was time for break. Oliver, Emma, and I walked over to the koi pond. The fence was already up, and we didn't see any signs of a snake.

Emma and I filled Oliver in about Thespis, and he surprised me with a snake fact.

"Did you know some toads will bloat themselves up so snakes can't swallow them?" he asked.

Is it too late to be a bloated toad for the performance? I wondered. *At least then I won't have to move in front of the audience.*

On Monday, Mom had a thrilling update. "I spoke with Deborah Aston, and we worked through the details. She'll be interviewing you all on Thursday afternoon. Thespis will be done with his antibiotics and ready for release by then, so they can capture that too."

Thursday afternoon? That was the day before our big drama camp performance. *Maybe the interview will give me more confidence before going onstage,* I thought hopefully.

The night before the interview I could hardly sleep! I kept practicing the speech I wanted to give.

Snakes help control unwanted pests and are an important part of the food chain for animals like coyotes, hawks, and owls. Snakes can become victims when people get scared because they don't know any better. We started our snake rescue club to help prevent that!

The interview could be the club's big break, I thought as I finally drifted off to sleep. I needed to be ready.

"Tomorrow is showtime. We're expecting a full house!" Divya said when we got to camp Thursday. "We're going to practice all day."

A full house? I thought.

My stomach felt like I'd eaten *a dozen* black-bean brownies. I hoped the interview that afternoon would help relieve some of my nerves. I reminded myself of Divya's words. *Practice makes perfect.*

Emma seemed to read my mind. "Are you excited about the interview?" she asked as she danced next to me.

"I just hope it goes well," I said. But my feet were as scattered as my thoughts. I bumped into Jordyn again. "Whoops, sorry."

"It's fine," Jordyn said in a soft voice. She didn't seem as confident as usual.

Divya stopped the music. "Keep trying your best. Don't start doubting yourselves! Let's take a short break."

"What's the deal with the interview?" Taylor asked when we'd all paused.

"It's happening this afternoon at my place," I said.

"Can I join y'all?" Oliver asked.

Taylor didn't wait for me to answer. "Sure," she said. "You should join us too, Jordyn."

"Maybe. I'll check with my dad," Jordyn replied.

I took a deep breath. Things were getting out of hand. Taylor and Jordyn didn't even like snakes. Emma looked at me with wide eyes.

The more the merrier, I reminded myself.

CHAPTER 9

DISASTER STRIKES

Snake fact #9: Snake venom can be used to make medications like antivenom, which can help in case of a venomous snake bite.

Emma, Taylor, Jordyn, and Oliver joined my family and me in our front yard that afternoon. We kicked a soccer ball while we waited for Deborah Aston to arrive for the interview.

I imagined a fancy van with the news logo arriving, but a cameraman driving a smart car showed up instead. He carried a tripod and a video camera with a microphone that looked like it was wrapped in a fluffy dog toy.

Deborah Aston climbed out of the car too. "Hi!" she said cheerfully. "Let's get started."

Mom and Dad stayed near the garage, pretending to organize a few things. I could tell they were listening in on the first part of the interview before we released Thespis.

"Why don't you all stand on the front porch with the taller kids in the back?" the cameraman said. "The lighting is good there."

The porch barely had any shade because of the afternoon sun. Nolan walked to the back, while Emma and I moved to the front. Oliver looked over at me like he was trying to compare heights and figure out where to go. Then Taylor stepped in front of him, and Jordyn joined her.

The cameraman perched the camera right on his shoulder.

"Why do you think snakes should be saved?" Deborah asked.

This was the moment I'd been practicing for! I opened my mouth to start my speech but . . .

"Snakes are awesome," Oliver said before I had a chance to answer.

Taylor cleared her throat. "But some people are afraid of snakes, even if they try not to be."

"Right," Jordyn said. She wobbled a little.

"Not everyone hates snakes, though," Emma said. "Girls can be interested in snakes too."

"People in our neighborhood were posting about snakes. They didn't know venomous ones from harmless ones," Nolan said.

"That's what I noticed. I wanted to fix that!" I said, practically shouting so I could jump in on the conversation.

"The club was Naomi's idea," Emma added.

I put my arm around her. "My friend Emma and her mom have done a great job—"

I didn't have a chance to finish my sentence because Jordyn wobbled again. Suddenly her knees gave out. She fell to the ground, pulling me down with her. Ouch!

Mom and Dad rushed over.

"Are you girls all right?" Dad asked us. He and Mom helped us get back on our feet.

I nodded. Jordyn started to tear up, which seemed really unlike her.

The cameraman stopped recording. Mom checked Jordyn over like she was one of her patients even though Mom only treated animals. She still knew a lot about medicine.

"How about some refreshments before we continue?" Dad said. In a matter of moments, he brought out a plate of homemade sugar cookies, a pitcher of lemonade, and cups for everyone.

"I think I should call my dad to pick me up," Jordyn said after a few sips of lemonade.

"Are you sure you don't want to stay for the snake release?" I asked.

Jordyn shook her head. She seemed even less confident than she had at camp earlier.

What's going on with her? I wondered.

"You can come play with Marshmallow while you check in with your dad," Taylor offered.

As much as Taylor wanted to be on the news, it was probably a good thing that she wouldn't be around when we released Thespis. It was bad enough that Jordyn and I had fallen down during the interview. Our club wouldn't seem legit if Taylor started screaming.

"I guess I'll see you tomorrow at camp for our big performance," I said before they left.

Jordyn's shoulders slumped. "Ugh. After today, I'm not sure I'm cut out for acting."

That wasn't the response I'd expected. Before I could say anything, Jordyn and Taylor headed across the street. Then Mom brought Thespis out in the carrier. The cameraman picked the camera back up and started to film again.

"This is a hognose snake that was found not too far from here," Mom said. "The club has been helping to rehabilitate him."

I held up my notebook to snake fact #279: *Releasing a snake in a familiar area will help increase its chances of survival.* The camera was probably too far back to read.

"I'm so proud of these kids for taking an interest in helping animals and the neighborhood," Mom continued. She looked right into the camera as she spoke, sounding polished and professional, unlike me. "Snakes play an important role in our ecosystem. And not to worry! The kids in the club are supervised and only help nonvenomous snakes."

"Our mom is a veterinarian and trained wildlife rehabilitator. Other people know her as Dr. Nash," Nolan added, sounding charming.

I should've said something like that, I thought.

Emma, Oliver, Nolan, and I crouched near the carrier as Mom opened it. Thespis didn't leave right away, so Mom pulled him out. He hissed and did another bluff strike.

I turned to the camera. "That was a fake strike. This little guy could win an award for being a good actor."

As Thespis slithered into the grass, I heard a bark. I turned to see Taylor walking Marshmallow in her front yard with Jordyn.

Marshmallow barked again and lunged forward. Like she'd done before, she slipped out of her harness and came bolting over to us. Taylor and Jordyn ran after her, but they weren't fast enough to catch her.

"What should we do?" Emma asked.

"We can't let Marshmallow grab the snake!" I said.

We made a shield around Thespis, but that made him stressed. The snake started to twirl in circles before spiraling onto his back. His mouth opened wide. Then his tongue flopped out.

Did he have a heart attack and die? I wondered.

Then his tongue flicked, and I knew he was just acting.

Marshmallow sprang forward, breaking through our legs before anyone could stop her. Nolan tried to grab her, but the puppy went right over to Thespis.

"Leave it, Marshmallow!" I yelled. This was bad! She could kill the snake.

Marshmallow looked over at me and wagged her tail. That gave Nolan just enough time to pull her away from the snake.

Taylor ran over to put the harness back on her dog. Then she turned to the camera. In all the commotion, I had forgotten it was there.

"Marshmallow is kind of the club mascot," Taylor said. "Naomi has been helping me teach her snake avoidance. It finally worked!"

Jordyn glanced over at the snake but ducked when the camera pointed at her.

"Thespis is like a zombie," Nolan said as the snake rolled over and started to move along.

"That was some performance!" Oliver said.

Everyone laughed, including Taylor. I couldn't believe it. She screamed over a plastic snake but laughed about a real one. People could be so surprising!

"Well, that's a wrap," Deborah said. "We got some great material. I can guarantee this will be the best assignment of my day."

"But wait! I have so much more I want to say," I said.

"We have to respect their time," Dad reminded me. He offered Deborah and the cameraman more cookies and lemonade before they left.

Everyone finished off the remaining treats and started playing soccer again. I didn't feel like playing. I sat down on the porch. The excitement of the day had burst like a balloon.

"You okay?" Mom asked, joining me.

I thought about everything that had happened. I was glad Marshmallow's training had paid off and Thespis had escaped safely. But the interview had been so awful. It definitely wouldn't make us famous enough to help our snakey mission.

"I wanted to be a champion for snakes, but I barely got to say a word," I complained, leaning into Mom. "And now I feel like a drama noodle."

Mom brushed away a strand of hair that was in my eyes. "Life takes unexpected turns that we can't always control. I hope you can look back on the interview and realize that things might've gone better than you think."

I curled up in my mom's arms. I wanted to believe her, but I couldn't help worrying.

If I can't ace an interview about something I care so much about, how am I going to ace performing in front of a full house? I wondered.

CHAPTER 10

PERFORMANCE TIME

Snake fact #10: People who collect venom from snakes
are called snake milkers. (No, snakes don't make milk
like cows!) Snake milkers have dangerous jobs—they hold
snakes against vials to collect venom.

The day of the drama camp performance,
I woke up just as worried.

"I can't believe Marshmallow actually
listened," Taylor said on the drive to camp.

"Her training paid off," I said. "I just didn't
think it would be the day of our interview."

Emma laughed and showed us a sketch
she'd done of Thespis coiled on his back with
his tail curled up and mouth hanging wide
open. "I'll never forget that moment!"

"Me neither," Taylor said. "Thanks again for helping me train Marshmallow."

"I still can't believe how calm you were yesterday," I said.

Taylor blushed. "I think the more experience I get with snakes, the less scary they'll be."

Told you so, I wanted to say. But it seemed like a comment that was better kept to myself.

"See you at the performance later. Break a leg, ladies!" Dad said when we got to camp.

I took a deep breath to calm my nerves.

Oliver ran over as soon as we arrived. "Have you seen a sneak peek of the interview?"

I cringed thinking about all the mishaps in the interview, like Jordyn and me falling and Marshmallow almost attacking Thespis.

"Not yet, but my mom said it'll air a week from today," I answered.

When Jordyn showed up, her shoulders were slumped. For a moment, I hesitated. Then I walked over to her. "You okay?"

Jordyn sighed. I didn't think she was going to say anything, but as I was about to give up and rejoin my friends, she blurted out, "I have stage fright, okay? I don't think I can perform today."

Stage fright? I thought.

I replayed the way Jordyn's legs had buckled and how she'd avoided the camera yesterday. It made a lot more sense now. It had never occurred to me that Jordyn and I might have something in common. She was nervous about speaking in public too!

"But drama is your life! You said so yourself. You're an amazing actress," I said, trying to keep my voice down.

Jordyn pulled her hair back into a ponytail. "I choked yesterday in front of the camera. What if that happens again today in front of everyone?"

"I'm not a natural at this drama camp stuff, but remember some of Divya's tips. How can you try to not give in to fear?" I asked her.

Jordyn put her hands on her hips. "Easy for you to say. You're not afraid of anything. You handle snakes!"

"If you want to know the truth, I was really upset about all the things that went wrong during the interview. But then I realized a lot went right—we shared some information, and we came together to save Thespis. With snakes, I guess I don't think about me. I focus on helping them," I said.

Jordyn twisted her lip like she was thinking.

"I get where you're coming from, though." I moved closer so no one could overhear my confession. "I'm afraid of getting onstage in front of everyone too."

Jordyn stared at me. "Really?"

"Cross my heart," I said.

Just then the other kids joined us. "What's going on?" Emma asked.

I decided to be brave. "I told Jordyn about how performing kind of scares me."

"It seems like we all have things we don't like or are afraid of," Taylor said.

She was right, I realized. Our fears didn't have to hold us back though.

Jordyn caught my eye, and I gave her a big thumbs-up.

Before I knew it, it was time for our performance. Divya smiled at us.

"I hope you've had a wonderful time at Acting Explorers Camp!" she said. "Remember to be in the moment and enjoy the spotlight."

As we made our way onto the stage, Alexandra greeted us. "Deborah said things went well with the interview. I can't wait to see the news clip as well as this performance!"

"Well, actually—" I started to say, but Divya urged us onto the stage.

The lights were so bright I started sweating, but then I found my mom and dad in the audience, along with Nolan. I waved at Emma's mom and Taylor's uncle.

While I waited for "The Wild Zoo" to start playing, I thought about inspiration and some of the things Divya had taught us. *Be you and be creative. Acting is really the art of reacting.*

I'd chosen to be an alligator because of what Jordyn had said. But if I was going to do something wild—like performing in front of everyone—I wanted to be *me*.

I pictured Thespis in my mind as I wiggled and slithered to the movements of the song.

I didn't care if anyone thought snakes were silly or my acting was a joke.

Jordyn gave me a thumbs-up now, and she got through every wolfy movement with ease. Emma, Taylor, and Oliver nailed their parts too! At the end of the song, the audience went wild with clapping and cheers.

"You all did amazing!" Divya said as she led us out into the audience. It was time to watch what the other kids in drama camp had been working on. "You've all grown so much."

Before I found my seat, Jordyn pulled me to the side. "I didn't pass out! Your advice really helped, Naomi. Sorry I judged you about the snake stuff. It's not my thing, but I should've been nicer that it's yours."

I smiled. "Thanks for saying that. To be honest, I didn't want to sign up for this camp, but I'm glad I did."

I meant it. Once I'd worked through my fear, camp had been fun. I'd gotten to spend time

with Emma and Taylor, plus made two new
friends and a lot of memories.

"Guess what I got?" Mom asked Sunday
morning while Dad served us sweet potato
pancakes.

"X-rays from a two-headed snake with two
hearts?" Nolan asked.

Mom chuckled. "No, but I'd love to see that."

"Have you been doing more snake
research again?" I asked, helping myself to
the cinnamon butter, brown sugar, and pecan
topping Dad had whipped up.

"Actually . . . Isla told me about two-headed
snakes with two hearts," Nolan said. His cheeks
looked red, but not like sunburn-red. "That girl
we met outside a couple weeks ago? I ran into
her at the library."

"That's awesome," I said around a mouthful
of fluffy pancake. Nolan had actually been
supportive of my acting stuff, and I wanted

to support him back. "I think it's great you're becoming a snake expert."

It didn't matter if he learned more than me or if I sat on the sidelines. That wasn't something to be afraid of. The more we all learned, the more we'd *all* be able to help snakes and our neighborhood. That's what mattered most to me.

"No more guesses? I got the link to the interview!" Mom said. She set up her tablet so we could watch it. I gulped as it loaded.

Deborah Aston sat at a news desk, looking professional in a blazer and colorful shirt. "Today on Feel Good Friday, check out these kids who have a unique mission," she said.

The video started playing on a screen next to her, and then the camera panned to the action of the snake release. The scenes were slightly out of order, and I realized lots of things had been cut.

"Snakes are awesome," Oliver's voice said during a clip of Thespis curling up.

It was great to see the little snake again, even just on screen. I hoped the hognose was living his best life now away from pools.

Next the camera moved to an image of me looking serious. Nolan's voice played over the top of the video. He talked about how our club had started. I held up my notebook, and the camera zoomed in so close I could see my snake facts!

Then the camera moved over to Emma, who said, "Girls can be interested in snakes too." The video featured pictures of Taylor, Emma, and Jordyn looking their strongest and best.

Mom gave her short, polished speech, and then the rest of the video played out, including the dramatic release as Thespis played dead and Marshmallow nearly grabbed him. It finished with Taylor mentioning that Marshmallow was kind of our mascot and how we'd been training the puppy to avoid snakes.

Finally, the camera returned to Deborah Aston in the news studio. "Snakes *do* play an important part in the environment even if we don't always appreciate their presence. I'm proud of these kids too for making a difference!"

Wow! I thought when the clip ended. The interview had turned out okay after all—with some editing.

"You and Nolan have always been famous in our eyes, but even more so now," Dad said with a wink.

"I can't wait for all of Austin to see this on Friday," Nolan said.

Same! I especially couldn't wait to show Emma and the rest of the crew, including our new friends. Our club was growing, and our message was really getting out there now. I knew more adventures were in store . . . though hopefully not quite so full of drama.

GLOSSARY

bluff (BLUFF)—a show of bravery that isn't true

commotion (kuh-MOH-shuhn)—noisy excitement and confusion

diurnal (dye-UR-nuhl)—active during the day and resting at night

ecosystem (EE-koh-sis-tuhm)—a system of living and nonliving things in an environment

improvisation (im-prov-uh-ZEY-shuhn)—the act or art of speaking or performing without practice or preparing ahead of time

mimic (MIM-ik)—to imitate the look, actions, or behaviors of another plant or animal

musk (MUHSK)—an oil some snakes produce when they sense danger

naturalist (NACH-er-uh-list)—a person who studies nature and especially plants and animals as they live in nature

omnivore (OM-nuh-vor)—an animal that eats both plants and other animals

rehabilitate (ree-huh-BIL-uh-tayt)—to return to health or activity

respiratory (RESS-pi-ruh-taw-ree)—related to the process of breathing

terrarium (tuh-RER-ee-uhm)—a usually glass container used for keeping plants or small animals, such as snakes, indoors

trauma (TRAW-muh)—a serious bodily injury

venomous (VEN-uhm-us)—able to produce a poison called venom

wildlife rehabilitator (WILDE-life ree-huh-bil-uh-TAY-tor)—a person whose job it is to care for injured, orphaned, or sick animals so they can be released back into the wild

TALK ABOUT IT!

1. Have you ever participated in a performance? Did you get the part you wanted? Did things go the way you planned? Talk about your experience.

2. Naomi learns that people can be surprising. Look back through the story and find a few instances in which characters acted in surprising ways. Discuss why you think they acted like that.

3. How did the various characters act during the interview and why? How would you feel about doing a television interview? What do you think you would talk about?

WRITE ABOUT IT!

1. Pick one of the secondary characters in this book—Emma, Taylor, or Jordyn—and rewrite a scene or interaction from that character's point of view. (For example, try writing the charades scene from Emma's perspective.)

2. Naomi makes new friends at camp. Look back through this story and make a list of qualities you think would make a good friend. Which characters have those qualities? Which qualities do you and your friends have?

3. Write an update to the ending of the story! How do the other characters respond to seeing the interview? How do things change for the snake club after it airs?

SNAKE SAFETY

Snakes, whether in nature or kept as pets, are more likely to bite if they feel threatened. Many venomous bites happen when someone tries to handle or kill a snake. Like Thespis, snakes may give warning signs before striking, including hissing and rattling their tails. Snakes might also puff up or play dead. Pay attention to these signs to prevent bites.

You might see a snake while you are out in nature. If you do, give the snake space, admire it from a distance, and let it move along. Do not handle any snake unless you can correctly identify it and confirm it is nonvenomous! If you step on a snake or find that you are very close, move away quickly. Remember: leave the snake alone, and it will leave you alone.

Research and learn more about snakes in your area by checking out field guides and books from your local library. You can also check out these websites to learn more about garter snakes and hognose snakes:

- *MN Department of Natural Resources: Common Garter Snake*
  dnr.state.mn.us/reptiles_amphibians/commongartersnake.html
- *BioKIDS Kids' Inquiry of Diverse Species: Common Garter Snake*
  biokids.umich.edu/critters/Thamnophis_sirtalis/
- *Savannah River Ecology Laboratory: Eastern Hognose Snake*
  srelherp.uga.edu/snakes/hetpla.htm

NAOMI'S FAVORITE SNAKE FACTS

1. Most snakes have teeth, but only venomous snakes have fangs. Snakes don't have teeth like molars because they don't chew their food like herbivores.

2. Venom is basically toxic snake spit that stuns or kills prey. Venom can help break down food for snakes to digest.

3. Snakes don't get sick from their own venom!

4. Some venomous snakes have hollow fangs. They're like needles that inject venom from a special gland. Other snakes have grooved fangs. They drip venom out when the snake holds on to bite.

5. Fangs can be at the front of a snake's mouth or in the back part of a snake's mouth. A snake called the stiletto snake has side fangs.

6. Snakes like vipers have fangs that fold up against the roof of their mouths when they're not biting something. Gaboon vipers have the longest fangs at around two inches!

7. Spitting cobras have holes in their fangs that they shoot toxic venom out of if they feel threatened.

8. Snakes have several teeth hiding out in their gums if they need to replace them, including fangs if the snake is venomous.

9. Snake venom can be used to make medications like antivenom, which can help in case of a venomous snake bite.

10. People who collect venom from snakes are called snake milkers. (No, snakes don't make milk like cows!) Snake milkers have dangerous jobs—they hold snakes against vials to collect venom.

ABOUT THE AUTHOR

photo credit: Michael Anderson

Jessica Lee Anderson is the author of more than 50 books for children. When not writing, she enjoys exploring nature and going on hikes with her husband, Michael, and their daughter, Ava. They've come across a variety of snakes in their travels, including a rattlesnake. Jessica was once afraid of snakes, but after learning more about these unique creatures, she's developed a deep appreciation for them. You can learn more about Jessica by visiting jessicaleeanderson.com.

ABOUT THE ILLUSTRATOR

photo credit: Alejandra Barajas

Alejandra Barajas has a degree in fine arts from Guanajuato University, but she found her true passion in children's book illustration. She loves all kinds of stories and believes that each one has the power to teach something new and valuable. Alejandra is almost always drawing—even in her free time—but when she's not, she can be found spending time with her family and dogs in Guanajuato, Mexico.